Three Pigs and a Gingerbread Man

Crabtree Publishing Company

www.crabtreebooks.com

1-800-387-7650

PMB 59051, 350 Fifth Ave.
59th Floor,
New York, NY 10118

616 Welland Ave.
St. Catharines, ON
L2M 5V6

Published by Crabtree Publishing in 2013

For Leah and Oliver

Series editor: Louise John
Editors: Katie Powell, Kathy Middleton
Notes to adults: Reagan Miller
Cover design: Paul Cherrill
Design: D.R.ink
Consultant: Shirley Bickler
Production coordinator and
    Prepress technician: Margaret Amy Salter
Print coordinator: Katherine Berti

Text © Hilary Robinson 2008
Illustration © Simona Sanfilippo 2008

First published in
2008 by Wayland
(A division of Hachette
Children's Books)

Printed in Canada
032016/CH20160307

Library and Archives Canada
Cataloguing in Publication

Robinson, Hilary, 1962-
        Three pigs and a gingerbread man / Hilary
Robinson ; illustrated by Simona Sanfilippo.

(Tadpoles: fairytale jumbles)
Issued also in electronic format.
ISBN 978-0-7787-8026-7 (bound).--ISBN 978-0-7787-8037-3 (pbk.)

        I. Sanfilippo, Simona II. Title. III. Series:
Tadpoles (St. Catharines, Ont.). Fairytale jumbles

PZ7.R6235Th 2012   j823'.914   C2012-904838-0

Library of Congress
Cataloging-in-Publication Data

Robinson, Hilary, 1962-
    Three pigs and a gingerbread man / written by
Hilary Robinson ; illustrated by Simona
Sanfilippo.
            p. cm. -- (Tadpoles: fairytale jumbles)
    Summary: Three pigs spend their days baking
and having fun until a wolf begins to pester them,
but the wolf is no match for their gingerbread
man.
        ISBN 978-0-7787-8026-7 (reinforced library
binding : alk. paper) -- ISBN 978-0-7787-8037-3
(pbk. : alk. paper) -- ISBN 978-1-4271-9149-6
(electronic pdf : alk. paper) -- ISBN 978-1-4271-
9157-1 (electronic html : alk. paper)
        [1. Stories in rhyme. 2. Characters in literature--
Fiction. 3. Wolves--Fiction. 4. Pigs--Fiction. 5.
Humorous stories.] I. Sanfilippo, Simona, ill. II.
Title.

PZ8.3.R575Thr 2012
[E]--dc23

                                                                2012027888

Three Pigs and a Gingerbread Man

Written by Hilary Robinson
Illustrated by Simona Sanfilippo

Crabtree Publishing Company

www.crabtreebooks.com

Three little pigs lived in Pig Yard
in a house made of red bricks.

They baked all day and had such fun,
'til a wolf began to play tricks!

He grinned and cried, "Little piggies,
it's a week since I last came to town..."

"...I thought I'd come to say sorry
that I blew your house of sticks down."

The wolf peered in through the window
as the three pigs mixed in a pan:
the flour, the sugar, the milk, and
the eggs to bake a gingerbread man.

The pigs shut the door of the oven
and looked the wolf in the eye.

"Beat it!" they cried. "If we let you in, you'll turn us into pork pie!"

The wolf was now getting angry
and ran to the door 'round the side.

He started ringing the doorbell,
"Quick!" said the pigs. "Let's hide."

"I'll huff, and I'll puff, and I'll blow your house down," growled the wolf, "But I'm weary today..."

"...so save me the trouble and open the
door, and I'll come in the easy way."

The Gingerbread Man heard all the fuss and banged on the hot oven door.

"Ready!" he cried. "I'm crispy and brown."
And he jumped down onto the floor.

"Hey, Gingerbread Man!" called
the wolf with a wink. "Would you
give me a hand to get in?"

"I won't let you in!" he shouted back.
"Not by the hair on my chinny chin chin!"

The Gingerbread Man stood there fearless,
as the wolf's hunger sharpened and grew.

"Go away, you big, greedy beast!
I know you'll eat me up, too!"

The wolf climbed up to the roof
of the house, and looked down
the chimney of bricks.

The Gingerbread Man cried, "Quick little pigs, let's light up a fire with sticks."

"That won't scare me," the mean wolf laughed, as he jumped down and looked about.

"I'll just find a bucket of water
to put your silly fire out."

The wolf leaped toward the three little pigs, as they shook with fear and fled.

But the Gingerbread Man came to
their rescue and kicked water all over
his head.

"Yes! Take that!" cried the Gingerbread Man, as the wolf fled from Pig Yard.

And the pigs lived happily ever after with the Gingerbread Man as...

...their guard!

Notes for adults

Tadpoles: Fairytale Jumbles are designed for transitional and early fluent readers. The books may also be used for read-alouds or shared reading with younger children.

Tadpoles: Fairytale Jumbles are humorous stories with a unique twist on traditional fairy tales. Each story can be compared to the original fairy tale, or appreciated on its own. Fairy tales are a key type of literary text found in the Common Core State Standards.

THE FOLLOWING BEFORE, DURING, AND AFTER READING SUGGESTIONS SUPPORT LITERACY SKILL DEVELOPMENT AND CAN ENRICH SHARED READING EXPERIENCES:

1. Make reading fun! Choose a time to read when you and the child are relaxed and have time to share the story.

2. Before reading, invite the child to preview the book. The child can read the title, look at the illustrations, skim through the text, and make predictions as to what will happen in the story. Predicting sets a clear purpose for reading and learning.

3. During reading, encourage the child to monitor his or her understanding by asking questions to draw conclusions, making connections, and using context clues to understand unfamiliar words.

4. After reading, ask the child to review his or her predictions. Were they correct? Discuss different parts of the story, including main characters, setting, main events, the problem and solution. If the child is familiar with the original fairy tale, invite he or she to identify the similarities and differences between the two versions of the story.

5. Encourage the child to use his or her imagination to create fairytale jumbles based on other familiar stories.

6. Give praise! Children learn best in a positive environment.

IF YOU ENJOYED THIS BOOK, WHY NOT TRY ANOTHER TADPOLES: FAIRYTALE JUMBLES STORY?

Hansel, Gretel and the Ugly Duckllng	*978-0-7787-1157-5 RLB* *978-1-4271-9229-5 Ebook (HTML)*	*978-0-7787-1166-7 PB* *978-1-4271-9305-6 Ebook (PDF)*
Snow White and the Enormous Turnip	*978-0-7787-8024-3 RLB* *978-1-4271-9158-8 Ebook (HTML)*	*978-0-7787-8035-9 PB* *978-1-4271-9150-2 Ebook (PDF)*
The Elves and the Emperor	*978-0-7787-8025-0 RLB* *978-1-4271-9159-5 Ebook (HTML)*	*978-0-7787-8036-6 PB* *978-1-4271-9151-9 Ebook (PDF)*
Goldilocks and the Wolf	*978-0-7787-8023-6 RLB* *978-1-4271-9156-4 Ebook (HTML)*	*978-0-7787-8034-2 PB* *978-1-4271-9148-9 Ebook (PDF)*
Rapunzel and the Billy Goats	*978-0-7787-1154-4 RLB* *978-1-4271-9226-4 Ebook (HTML)*	*978-0-7787-1158-2 PB* *978-1-4271-9302-5 Ebook (PDF)*
Beauty and the Pea	*978-0-7787-1155-1 RLB* *978-1-4271-9227-1 Ebook (HTML)*	*978-0-7787-1159-9 PB* *978-1-4271-9303-2 Ebook (PDF)*
Cinderella and the Beanstalk	*978-0-7787-1156-8 RLB* *978-1-4271-9228-8 Ebook (HTML)*	*978-0-7787-1161-2 PB* *978-1-4271-9304-9 Ebook (PDF)*

VISIT WWW.CRABTREEBOOKS.COM FOR OTHER CRABTREE BOOKS.